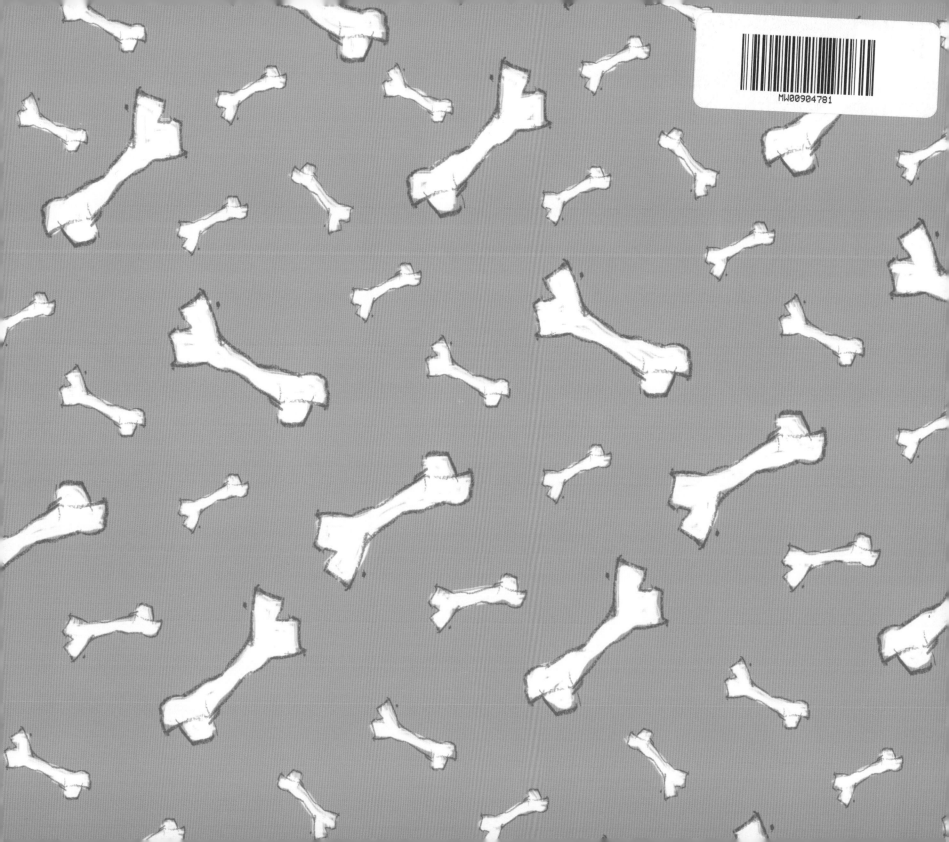

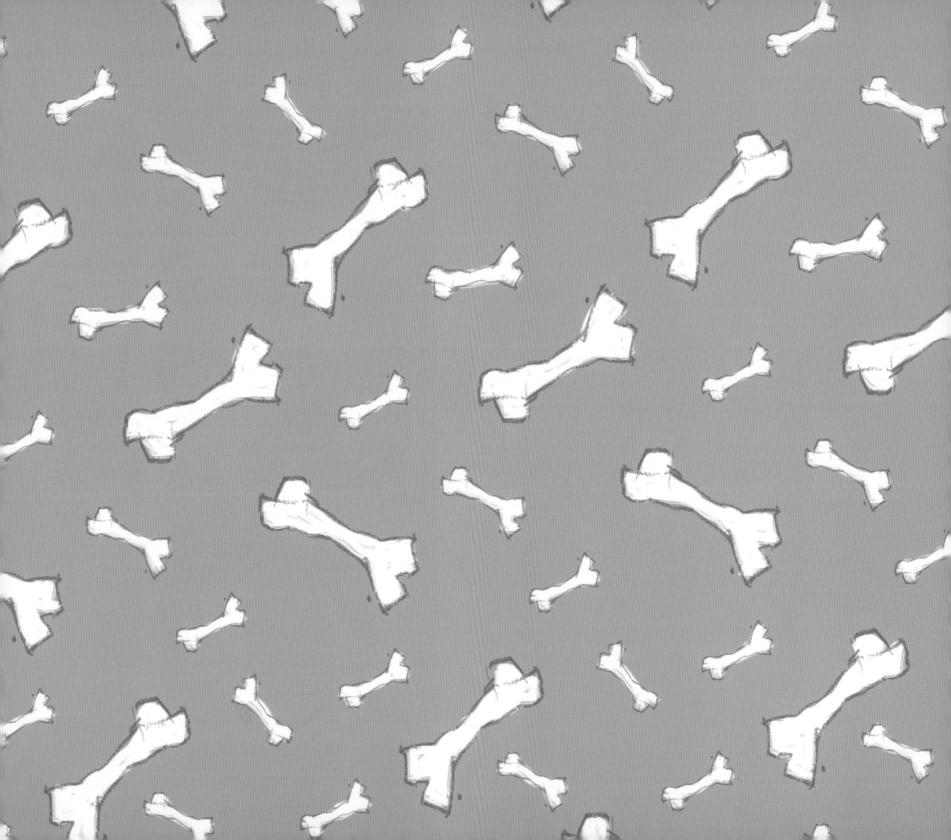

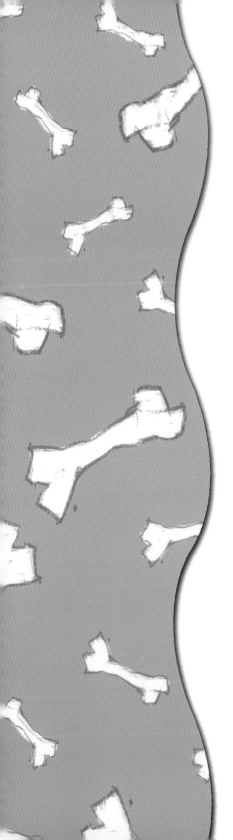

My DOGGIE Brought to Me

By Pam Schiller • Illustrated by Robert Sanford

Hi, I'm Noodlebug. Are you ready to "use your noodle?" Your "noodle" is your brain. You use it when you read or listen to stories.

Here's a story about a very busy doggie. I join her on one of the pages. See if you can find me!

School Specialty Publishing

Text © 2006 Noodlebug Productions LLC.
Art and Design © 2006 School Specialty Publishing.
Published by School Specialty Publishing, a member of the School Specialty Family.

Printed in the United States of America. All rights reserved. Except as permitted under the United States Copyright Act, no part of this publication may be reproduced or distributed in any form or by any means, or stored in a database retrieval system, without prior written permission from the publisher.

Noodlebug and all related logos and characters are registered trademarks of Noodlebug Productions LLC. Library of Congress Cataloging-in-Publication Data is on file with the publisher.

Send all inquiries to School Specialty Publishing • 8720 Orion Place • Columbus, OH 43240-2111

ISBN 0-7696-4276-4

1 2 3 4 5 6 7 8 PHXBK 11 10 09 08 07 06

On the first day of summer,
my doggie brought to me...

a branch from a sycamore tree.

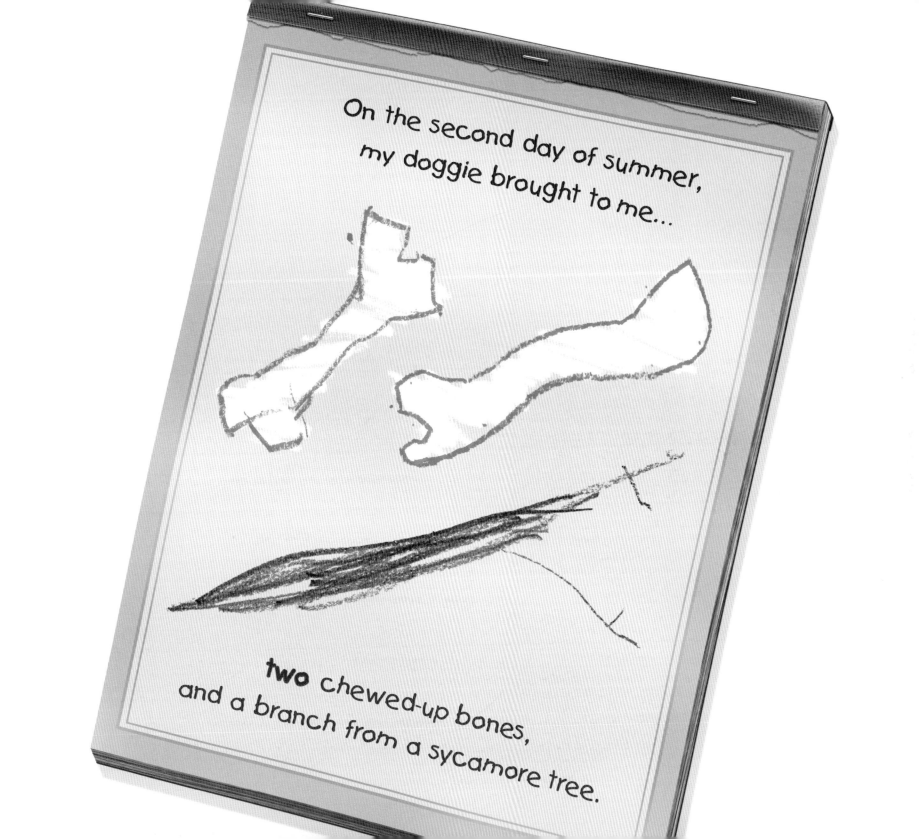

On the third day of summer,
my doggie brought to me...

three squeaky toys, **two** chewed-up bones,
and a branch from a sycamore tree.

On the fourth day of summer, my doggie brought to me...

four bouncing balls,
three squeaky toys, **two** chewed-up bones,
and a branch from a sycamore tree.

On the fifth day of summer,
my doggie brought to me...

five playful puppies, four bouncing balls,
three squeaky toys, two chewed-up bones,
and a branch from a sycamore tree.

How about something for you?"

Sharing is fun—try it! You'll feel as happy as the dog in this story.
Next time, try singing the words to the tune
"The Twelve Days of Christmas." Singing is good for your brain,
and it helps make things easier to remember.
See you again soon, and don't forget to "use your noodle!"

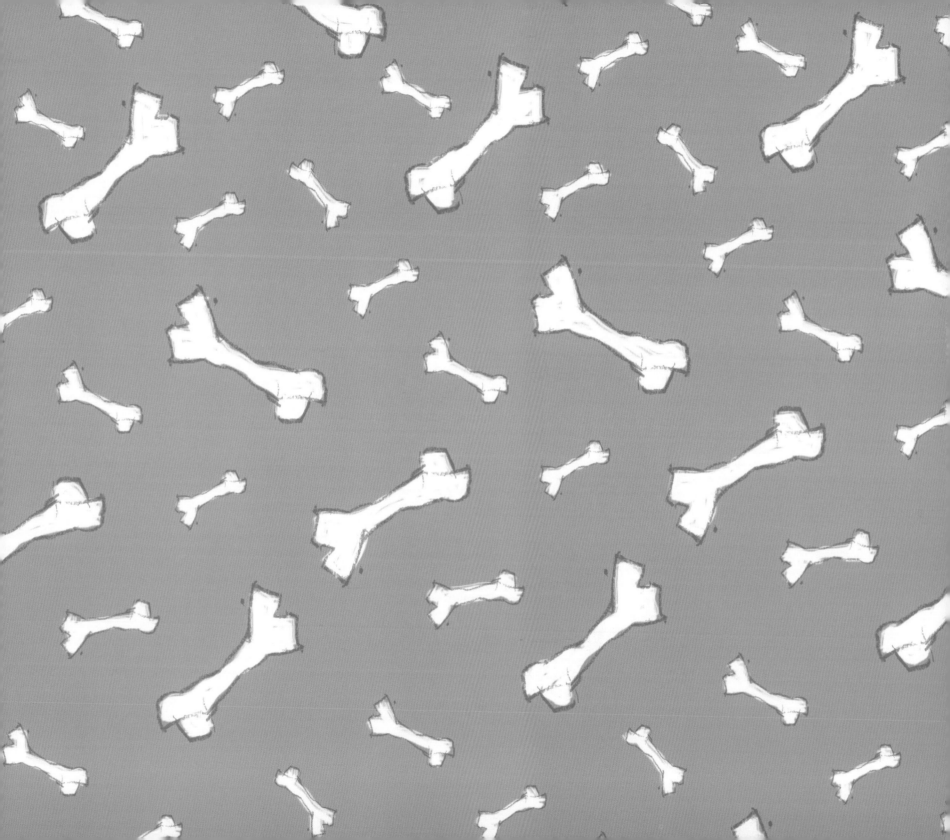

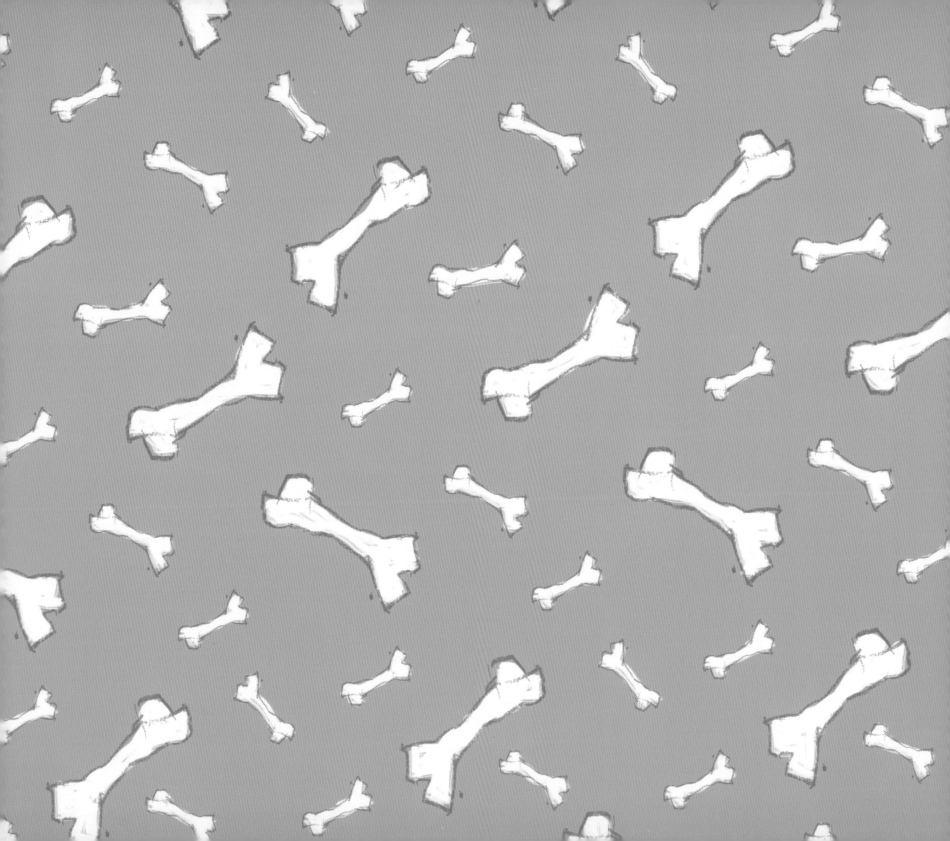